KV-198-388

Tom Sawyer at Play

and other toy stories

Compiled by Tig Thomas

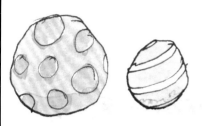

First published in 2014 by Miles Kelly Publishing Ltd
Harding's Barn, Bardfield End Green, Thaxted, Essex, CM6 3PX, UK

Copyright © Miles Kelly Publishing Ltd 2014

2 4 6 8 10 9 7 5 3 1

Publishing Director Belinda Gallagher
Creative Director Jo Cowan
Editorial Director Rosie Neave
Senior Editor Sarah Parkin
Senior Designer Joe Jones
Production Manager Elizabeth Collins
Reprographics Stephan Davis, Jennifer Hunt, Thom Allaway

All rights reserved. No part of this publication may be reproduced, stored in a retrieval system, or transmitted by any means, electronic, mechanical, photocopying, recording or otherwise, without the prior permission of the copyright holder.

ISBN 978-1-78209-466-1

Printed in China

British Library Cataloguing-in-Publication Data
A catalogue record for this book is available from the British Library

ACKNOWLEDGEMENTS

The publishers would like to thank the following artists who have contributed to this book:

Advocate Art: Milena Jahier, Claire Keay (inc. cover), Kimberley Scott
Beehive Illustration: Rupert Van Wyk (inc. decorative frames)

Made with paper from a sustainable forest

www.mileskelly.net   info@mileskelly.net

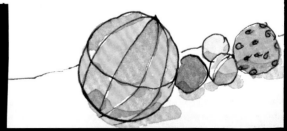

Contents

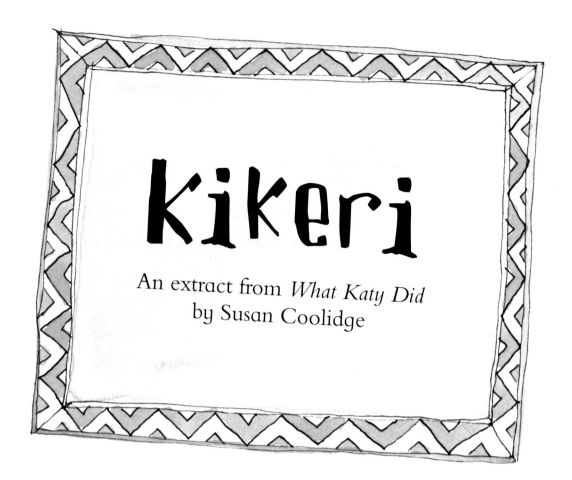

kikeri

An extract from *What Katy Did*
by Susan Coolidge

Katy Carr is part of a large family. Her brothers are Phil and Dorry, and her sisters are Clover, Elsie and John (short for Joanna). The children are looked after by their Aunt Izzie, who is kind but strict. The smaller children sleep together in the nursery.

THIS PARTICULAR MONDAY was rainy, so there couldn't be any outdoor play. Philly was not well and had been taking medicine. It was a great favourite with Aunt Izzie, who kept a bottle of it always on

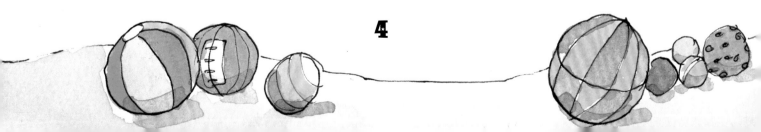

hand. The bottle was large and black, and the children shuddered at the sight of it.

After Philly had stopped roaring and spluttering, and play had begun again, the dolls were taken ill also. And so was Pikery, John's little yellow chair, which she always pretended was a doll too. John kept an old apron tied on Pikery's back.

Now, as she told the others, Pikery was very sick indeed. He must have some medicine, just like Philly.

"Give him some water," suggested Dorry.

"No," said John, "it must be black and out of a bottle, or it won't do any good."

After thinking a moment, she trotted quietly across the passage into Aunt Izzie's room. The children were enchanted when

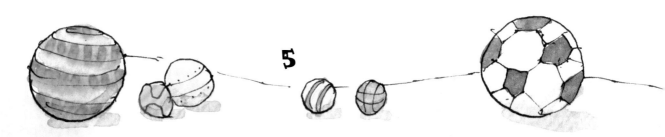

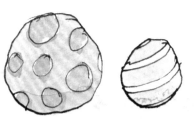

she marched back, the bottle in one hand, the cork in the other, and proceeded to pour a dose onto Pikery's wooden seat, which John called his lap.

"There! There!" she said. "Swallow it down – it'll do you good."

Just then Aunt Izzie came in. To her dismay she saw a trickle of something dark and sticky running down onto the carpet. It was Pikery's medicine, which he had refused to swallow.

"What is that?" she asked sharply.

"My baby is sick," faltered John, displaying the guilty bottle.

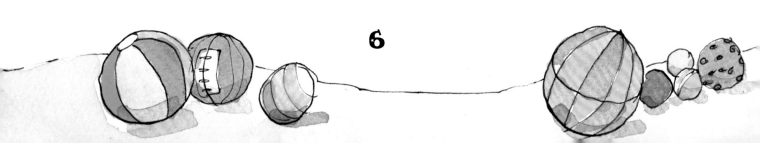

She scolded them and declared they were troublesome children, who couldn't be trusted one moment out of sight, and that she was more than half sorry she had promised to go out that evening. "How do I know that before I come home you won't have set the house on fire?" she said.

"Oh, no we won't!" whined the children. But ten minutes afterwards they had forgotten all about it.

Supper passed off successfully, Aunt Izzie went out, and all might have gone well, had it not been that after their lessons, the children fell to talking about Kikeri.

Kikeri was a game they had invented themselves. It was a sort of mixture of Blindman's Buff and Tag – only instead of

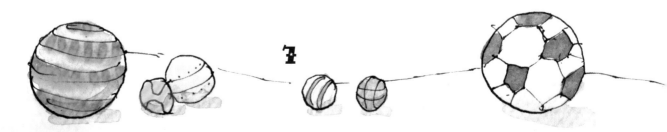

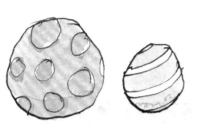

anyone's eyes being blindfolded, they all played in the dark.

One of the children would stay out in the hall, which was dimly lit from the stairs, while the others hid themselves in the nursery. When they were all hidden, they would call out "Kikeri" as a signal for the one in the hall to come in and find them.

Coming from the light he could see nothing, while the others could see only dimly. It was very exciting to stand in a corner, watching the dark figure stumbling about and feeling to the right and left.

Every now and then somebody, just escaping his clutches, would slip past into the hall, which was Freedom Castle, with a joyful shout of "Kikeri, Kikeri, Kikeri, Ki!"

Whoever was caught had to take the place of the catcher. Talking of it now put it into their heads to want to try it again.

So they all went upstairs. Dorry and John, though half undressed, were allowed to join the game. Philly was fast asleep in another room.

It was certainly splendid fun. Once Clover climbed up onto the mantelpiece and sat there, and when Katy, who was the catcher, groped about a little more wildly than usual, she caught hold of Clover's foot, and couldn't imagine where it came from. Another time Katy's dress caught on the bureau handle and was torn. But these were too much affairs of every day to interfere with the pleasures of playing Kikeri.

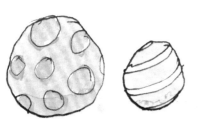

The fun seemed to grow greater the longer they played. In the excitement, time went on much faster than any of them dreamed. Suddenly, in the midst of the noise, there came a sound – the sharp, distinct slam of the door at the side entrance. Aunt Izzie had returned.

The dismay and confusion of that moment! Aunt Izzie was on her way up stairs! Katie scuttled off to her own room, where she went to bed with all possible speed. But the others found it much harder to go to bed – there were so many of them, all getting into each other's way, and with no lamp to see by.

Aunt Izzie, coming in with a candle in her hand, gave Clover a sharp scolding.

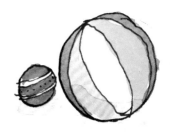

Then Aunt Izzie went to the bed where John and Dorry lay, fast asleep, and snoring as loudly as they knew how. Something strange in the appearance of the bed made her look more closely – she lifted the clothes, and there, sure enough, they were half dressed and with their school shoes on.

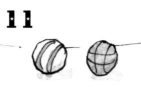

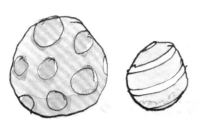

John and Dorry were forced to wake up, be scolded and made ready for bed.

Katy did not even pretend to be asleep when Aunt Izzie went to her room. Her conscience had woken up, and she was lying in bed, very miserable at the failure of setting an example to the younger ones.

The next day, Papa called them together and made them understand that Kikeri was not to be played any more. It was so seldom that Papa forbade any games, however boisterous, that this order really made an impression on the children. They never have played Kikeri again, from that day to this.

Playing at Jungle Book

An extract from *The Wouldbegoods*
by E Nesbit

*The Bastable children, Oswald, Dora, Dicky, Alice, Noel
and H.O., are staying with their father's friend, who they call
'the uncle'. Two timid children, Daisy and Denny, are staying
with them. A beer stand is a wooden frame to hold a beer barrel.*

NEXT MORNING, when we were having
breakfast, Oswald suddenly said,
"I know, we'll have a jungle in the garden!"
Then he continued, "We'll play Jungle
Book! I shall be Mowgli and the rest of you

13

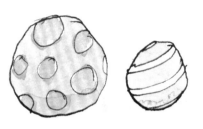

can be what you like."

We all agreed to make the jungle first and dress up for our parts afterwards. Of course, the shrubbery was to be the jungle, and the lawn under the cedar would be a forest glade. And then we began to collect the things.

We all thought of different things. First we dressed up pillows in the skins of beasts and set them about on the grass to look as natural as we could. Denny helped with the wild beast skins, and said, "Please may I make some paper birds to put in the trees? I know how."

Of course we all said yes, and so timid Denny quickly made quite a lot of large paper birds with red tails. But while he was

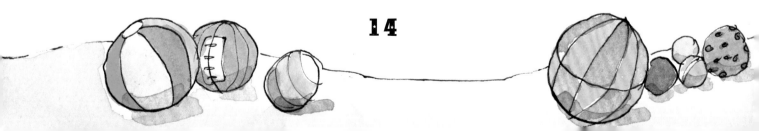

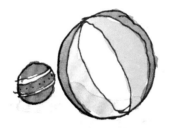

doing this he suddenly said, or rather screamed, "Oh?"

We looked and it was a creature with great horns and a fur rug – something like a bull and also something like a minotaur – and I don't wonder Denny was frightened. But it was only Alice, and it was first-class.

Oswald undid the back of the glass case in the hall, and got out the stuffed fox with the green and grey duck in its mouth. When the others saw how awfully life-like

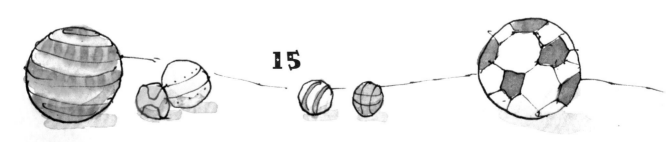

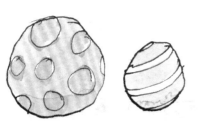

they looked on the lawn, they all rushed off to fetch the other stuffed things. The uncle really has a tremendous lot of stuffed animals. The duck-bill – what's its name? – looked very well sitting on his tail with the otter snarling at him.

Then Dicky got the hose and put the end over a branch of the cedar tree. We got the step ladder they clean windows with, and let the hose rest on the top of the ladder. Then we got Father's and the uncle's raincoats and covered the step ladder with them, so that the water from the hose ran down in a stream, away across the grass. The stuffed otter and duck-bill-thing looked just as if they were in their native haunts!

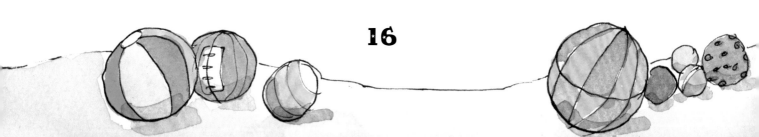

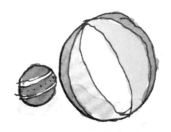

I do hope all of this is not very dull to read about. I know it was jolly good fun for us to do.

We got all the rabbits out of their hutches and put pink paper tails on them. They got away somehow, and before they were caught the next day, they had eaten a good many lettuces and other things.

Denny put paper tails on the guinea pigs. One of the guinea pigs was never seen again, and the same could be said for the tortoise, after we had painted his shell a brilliant red. He crawled away and returned no more.

The lawn under the cedar was transformed into a dream of beauty, what with all of the stuffed animals, the waterfall

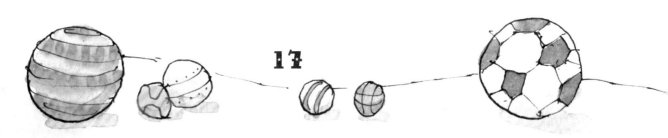

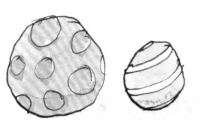

and the pink paper-tailed rabbits and guinea pigs.

Alice said, "I wish the tigers did not look so flat." For of course with pillows you can only pretend it is a sleeping tiger, not one getting ready to make a spring out at you. It is very difficult to prop up tiger skins in a life-like manner when there are no bones inside them.

"What about the beer stands?" I said. And so we got two out of the cellar, and with string we fastened them to the tigers – they were really fine.

Then H. O. painted his legs and his hands to make himself brown, so that he might be Mowgli. Although Oswald had clearly said earlier that he was going to be

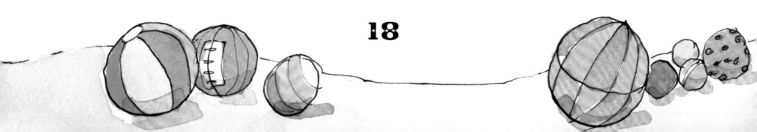

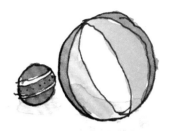

Mowgli himself.

Of course the others weren't going to stand that. So Oswald said, "Very well. Nobody asked you to brown yourself like that. But now you've done it, you've got to go and be a beaver, and live in the dam under the waterfall."

Noel said, "Don't make him. Let him be the bronze statue that the fountain plays out of."

So we let him have the hose and hold it up over his head. It made a lovely fountain.

Then Dicky and Oswald and I did ourselves brown too. The brown did not come off any of us for days.

Oswald was to be Mowgli, and we were just beginning to arrange the different parts.

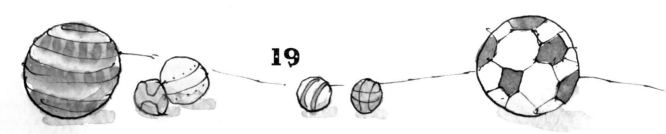

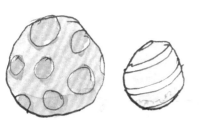

The rest of the hose that was on the ground was Kaa, the python. While most of us were talking, Dicky and Noel got messing about with the beer stand tigers.

And then a really sad event instantly occurred, which was not really our fault.

That Daisy girl had been mooning indoors all the afternoon, and now she suddenly came out, just as Dicky and Noel had got under the tigers and were shoving them along to frighten each other. They did look jolly like real tigers.

As soon as Daisy saw the tigers she stopped short, and fell flat on the ground.

Then we were truly frightened. Dora and Alice lifted her up, and her mouth was a violet colour and her eyes were half shut.

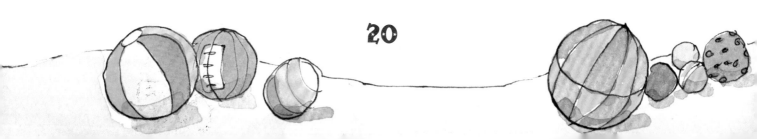

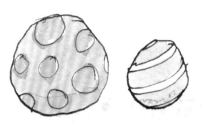

We did what we could. We rubbed her hands. And we were all doing what we could as hard as we could, when we heard the click of the front gate.

There were feet on the gravel, and there was the uncle's voice, saying in his hearty manner, "This way. This way."

And then, without further warning, the uncle, three other gentlemen and two ladies burst upon the scene.

Us boys had no clothes on. We were all wet through. Daisy was in a faint or a fit, or dead, none of us then knew which. And all the stuffed animals were there. Most of them had got a sprinkling, and the otter and the duck-bill-thing were simply soaked. And some of us were painted dark brown!

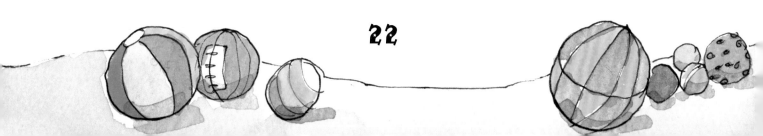

"What's all this?" said the uncle.

Oswald spoke up and said it was Jungle Book we were playing, and he didn't know what was up with Daisy. He explained as well as anyone could.

When Father came home we got a good talking to, and we said we were sorry, especially about Daisy. We promised that in the future we would be good.

It turned out Daisy was not really dead at all. It was only fainting.

I have not even told you half the things we did for the jungle – for instance, about sofa cushions and the uncle's fishing boots!

Tom Sawyer at Play

An extract from *The Adventures of Tom Sawyer*
by Mark Twain

*Tom lives in Mississippi in the nineteenth century. He believes
in superstitions and magic, and here he is trying to work a spell to
make his lost marbles come back. Joe Harper is a friend of his and
they like playing at Robin Hood. A shingle is a wooden roof tile.*

HE WENT TO A ROTTEN log near at
hand, and began to dig under one
end of it with his knife. He soon struck
wood that sounded hollow. Tom put his
hand there and uttered this incantation:

24

"What hasn't come here, come! What's here, stay here!"

Then Tom scraped away the dirt, exposing a pine shingle. He took it up and uncovered a shapely little treasure house, whose bottom and sides were of shingles. In it lay a marble. Tom's astonishment was boundless! He scratched his head and said, "Well, that beats anything!"

Then Tom tossed the marble away and stood thinking. The truth was, a superstition of his had failed here. If you buried a marble with certain necessary incantations, left it alone for a fortnight, and then opened the place with the incantation he had just used, you would find that all the marbles you had ever lost had gathered themselves

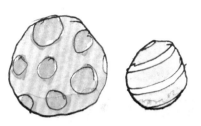

together in that place.

But now, this thing had actually failed. Tom's faith was shaken. He had many a time heard of this thing succeeding, but never of its failing before. It did not occur to Tom that he had tried it several times before, himself, but could never find the hiding-places afterwards.

Tom puzzled over the matter for some time, and finally decided that some witch had interfered and broken the charm, so he gave up discouraged. But it occurred to him that he might as well have the marble he had just thrown away, and he went and made a patient search for it. But he could not find it.

Now he went back to his treasure house

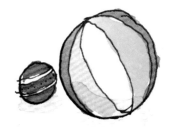

and carefully placed himself just as he had been standing when he tossed the marble away. Then he took another marble from his pocket and tossed it in the same way, saying, "Brother, go find your brother!"

Tom watched where it stopped, and went there and looked. But the marble must have fallen short or gone too far, so he tried twice more. The last repetition was successful – two marbles lay within a foot of each other.

Just then the blast of a toy tin trumpet came faintly down the green aisles of the forest. Tom flung off his jacket and trousers, turned his scarf into a belt, raked away

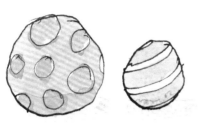

some brush behind the rotten log to uncover a bow and arrow, a wooden sword and a tin trumpet, and in a moment had seized these things and bounded away, barelegged, with a fluttering shirt.

He presently halted under a great elm, blew an answering blast, and then began to tiptoe and look warily out, this way and that. He said cautiously, to an imaginary company, "Hold, my merry men! Keep hidden until I blow."

Now Joe Harper appeared, dressed and armed like Tom.

"Hold! Who comes here into Sherwood Forest without my pass?" Tom called.

"Guy of Guisborne wants no man's pass. Who art thou that – that—"

"Dares to hold such language," said Tom, prompting him, for they talked by the book from memory.

"Who art thou that dares to hold such language?" Joe said.

"I, indeed! I am Robin Hood, as thy carcass soon shall know," replied Tom.

"Then art thou indeed that famous outlaw?" said Joe. "Right gladly will I dispute with thee the passes of the merry wood. Have at thee!"

They took their swords, dumped their other traps on the ground, struck a fencing attitude, foot to foot, and began a grave, careful combat, two up and two down.

Presently Tom said, "Now, if you've got the hang of it, go at it lively!"

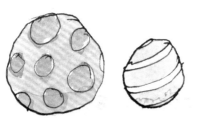

So they went at it lively, panting and perspiring with the work. By and by Tom shouted, "Fall! Fall! Why don't you fall?"

"I won't! Why don't you fall yourself? You're getting the worst of it," Joe replied.

"Why, that ain't anything. I can't fall, that ain't the way it is in the book. The book says, 'Then with one back-handed stroke he slew poor Guy of Guisborne.' You're to turn around and let me hit you in the back."

There was no getting around the authorities, so Joe turned, received the whack and fell.

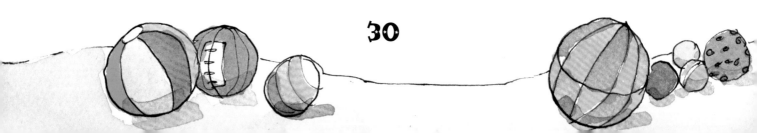

"Now," said Joe, getting up, "you've got to let me kill you. That's fair."

"Why, I can't do that, it ain't in the book."

"Well, it's blamed mean – that's all."

"Well, Joe, you can be Friar Tuck or Much the miller's son, and hit me with a quarter-staff – or I'll be the Sheriff of Nottingham and you be Robin Hood a little while and kill me."

This was satisfactory, and so these adventures were carried out. Then Tom became Robin Hood again, and was allowed, by the treacherous nun, to bleed his strength away through his neglected wound.

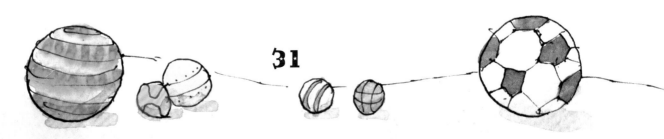

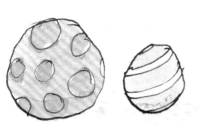

At last, Joe, representing a whole tribe of weeping outlaws, dragged him sadly forth, gave his bow into his feeble hands, and Tom said, "Where this arrow falls, there bury poor Robin Hood under the greenwood tree." Then he shot the arrow and fell back. He would have died, but he fell on a nettle and sprang up too gaily for a corpse!

The boys dressed themselves and went off grieving that there were no outlaws any more. They said they would rather be outlaws for a year in Sherwood Forest than President of the United States forever.

The Racketty-Packetty House in Trouble

An extract from *The Racketty-Packetty House*
by Frances Hodgson Burnett

*The dolls who live in the Racketty-Packetty House are always
scared of being thrown away. But the good fairy who tells this story
looks after them very well. One day one of the dolls, Ridiklis, brings
news for the other dolls that their owner, Cynthia, has gone away.*

"**THE DUCHESS TOLD ME,**" she said,
slowly, because it was bad news. "The
Duchess said that Cynthia went away,
because her Mamma had sent for her to tell
her that a little princess is coming to see her

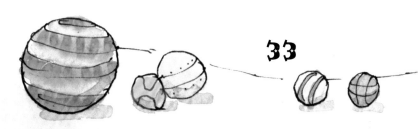

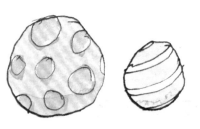

tomorrow. Cynthia's Mamma used to be a maid of honour to the Queen and that's why the little Princess is coming. The Duchess said—" and here Ridiklis spoke very slowly indeed, "that the nurse said she must tidy up the nursery, and have that Racketty-Packetty old dolls' house burned early tomorrow morning."

Meg, Peg, Gustibus and Kilmanskeg clutched at their hearts and gasped.

You can just imagine what a sad night it was. They went all over the house together, looking at every hole in the carpet, every broken window and every ragged blanket.

Now here is where I come in again – Queen Crosspatch – who is telling you this story. I always come in just at the nick of

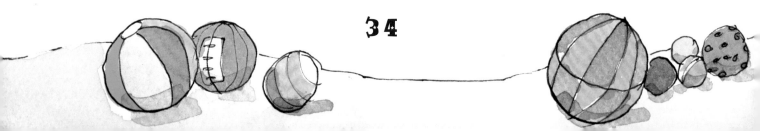

time when people like the Racketty-Packetty dolls are in trouble.

A whole army of my working fairies began to swarm in at the nursery window. The nurse was working very hard to tidy things, and she had not sense enough to see fairies at all. As soon as she made one corner tidy, they ran after her and made it untidy. The nurse could not make the nursery tidy and she was so flurried she forgot all about Racketty-Packetty House. And there it was when the little Princess came.

The Princess

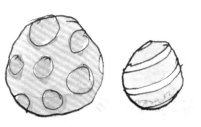

was a nice child, and was very polite to Cynthia when she showed her all her dolls, and her new dolls' house, Tidy Castle. But the Princess had so many grand dolls' houses in her palace that Tidy Castle did not surprise her at all. It was just when Cynthia was finding this out that I gave the order to my working fairies.

"Push the armchair away very slowly, so that no one will know it is being moved."

So they moved it away – very, very slowly. The next minute the little Princess gave a delightful start.

"Oh! What is that!" she cried out, hurrying towards the house.

Cynthia blushed all over. The Racketty-Packetty dolls tumbled down in a heap.

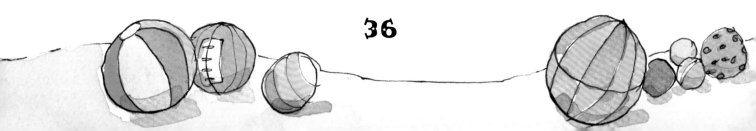

"It is only a shabby old dolls' house, your Highness," Cynthia stammered. "It belonged to my Grandmamma. I thought you had had it burned, Nurse!"

"Burned!" the little Princess cried out. "Why if it was mine, I wouldn't have it burned for worlds! Oh! Please push the chair away and let me look at it." And when the armchair was pushed aside, she scrambled down onto her knees.

"Oh!" she said. "How funny and dear! What a darling old dolls' house. It is shabby and needs mending, but it is almost exactly like one my Grandmamma had – she only let me look at it as a great treat."

Cynthia gave a gasp, for the Princess' Grandmamma had been the Queen.

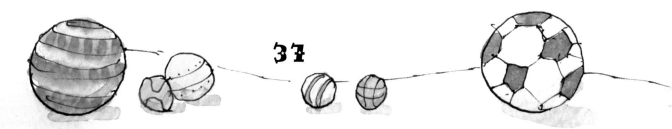

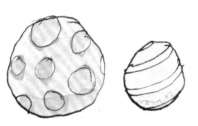

The little Princess picked up Meg and Peg and Kilmanskeg and Gustibus and Peter Piper as if they had really been a Queen's dolls.

"Oh! The darling dears," she said. "Look at their nice faces and their funny clothes. Just like Grandmamma's dolls' clothes. Oh! How I should like to dress them again just as they used to be dressed, and have the house all made just as it used to be when it was new."

"That old Racketty-Packetty House," said Cynthia, in shock.

"If it were mine I should make it just like

Grandmamma's, and I should love it more than any dolls' house I have. I never saw anything as nice and laughing and good natured as these dolls' faces. They look as if they have been having fun ever since they were born. Oh! If you were to burn them and their home I could never forgive you!"

"I never – never – will – your Highness," stammered Cynthia.

As the Princess liked Racketty-Packetty House so much, Cynthia gave it to her for a present. The Princess was really happy, and before she went she made a little speech to the whole Racketty-Packetty family.

"You are going to come and live with me," she said. "And you shall all be dressed beautifully again. Your house shall be

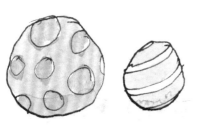

mended and made as lovely as ever it was." Then she was gone.

Every bit of it came true. Racketty-Packetty House was carried to a splendid nursery in a palace. Meg and Peg and Kilmanskeg and Ridiklis and Gustibus and Peter Piper were made so gorgeous that if they had not been so nice they would have grown proud. But they didn't.

The dolls in the other dolls' houses used to make deep curtsies when a Racketty-Packetty doll passed them. Peter Piper could scarcely stand it, because it always made him want to stand on his head and laugh!